AF 131935

Sweat oozed
from a
cross held high
in hand

Another leaking and escaping (*) novel

(*) or '*escapista*', it's up to you.

© 2023, Miguel S.RUIZ
Édition : BoD - Books on Demand, info@bod.fr
Impression : BoD – Books on Demand,
In de Tarpen 42, Norderstedt (Allemagne)
Impression à la demande
ISBN : 978-2-3224-7149-2
Dépôt légal : Août 2023

Miguel S. Ruiz

Sweat oozed from a cross held high in hand

To everyone in particular –
and no one in general.

My attention was fixed on the more or less partial
sentences which, in complete solitude, at the
approach of sleep (*), become perceptible to the mind -
without any possibility to discover in them a prior
determination. These sentences, remarkably colorful
and with a perfectly correct syntax (**), appeared
to me as first class poetic elements.

(André Breton, « Les Pas Perdus »)

I don't know what I want but I know how to get it.

(John Lydon/Rotten)

(*) For the author, upon awakening.
(**) If not, blame the translator...

9

CONTENTS

Chapter I

Biting irony on a bench of

of bright fishes

The blissful *Trissotins* from Penthièvre St., gloomy accountants

hampered by gonorrhea, turn out to be the culprits of their

dismissals – yes, yes… So : implicit consent of two mute nostrils

(and their agony) or pink Gestapo clouds ? Be that as it may, we

were dealing with a concrete mirage. Let me explain to you : Muriel

and her moujik, in their own frozen furnace, bet everything on the

bride's petticoats brought to heel… Astride the world, their irony

risked filtering boulevards – not to mention the beautiful

grenadine ! Prostrate on a candle, the psychiatrist and his friends

waved two teapots and 5 wagons in an equivocal manner.

What for ? Because the orthodoxy of void struggles to replace the

knife of giraffes... And the tenderness of wild boars. Is it clear ?!?

$\mathbf{A}$ yellowish trout taking the chill on her knees wondered how

long she could still hold out before her illness knocked her down.

Kind Jean Nohain – carved out of a toothpick – brought him thirty

remedies with a concrete base of lava and immodesty. She

swallowed them with a good heart, but she took it badly : it was

Karl Marx's Duck Soup. "Pretty little purple lizard but

unremarkable, can you show me the way to the desert ?" we heard

then, in the distance... Well, can you imagine that I have since

enjoyed the sight of steering wheels and padded skai, those

that the latter offered me, naked. And my reaction-response was

without appeal : "You will recognize me from now on by my

haughty look, son of the razor !"

Quite often Marion Cotillard, with a knife-like face, runs First of

the Mohicans through a karcher. For personal convenience of

course, but no doubt also for a more specific purpose. Sigismond

Freud, in order to shut up Emily Jung's people, had gotten

into the habit of pulling a very juicy red bear out of his hat. Must

say that around Jeffrey Lee Pierce, he had always advocated playing

Catenaccio. From then on, realizing that he had exhausted all his

package, the teenager we are talking about began to regret having

bought a breviary on Amazon (it was that of a priest defrocked in

absentia). But here we are, in the end we won't care a bit : when we

are intimate, twenty thousand leagues under the 4 mothers, &

the giants' Index will finally launch the fishing net – for wanting

more ! And eighteen giraffes completely gone – for instance those

of Jacques Mesrine – will then necessarily go to join the idiot of the

15

sticky village, on Olympus (NB: this applies both to the very village

and to the aforementioned idiot). Stanley Kubrick and Germain

Nouveau will then lay their hands on a boulevardier virus, pressed

as they will be by fairly commercial things – admittedly friendly but

covered in blood. And Miou-Miou (on the crenellated ramparts of

Warsaw) will shadow a bird of misfortune rolled in flour.

Conclusion : she is very lucky to live in the Marais (Pontins) !

Yes monarchs appearing out of nowhere, I did murder the rotten

monkey. And all that to switch to Video Gag, compose a ritornello

and accuse some rambunctious Inuit of… disinformation. Henri (&

Olivier) Poupon, they squeaked and complained, as usual, of not

getting anywhere... "Poor idiots, get your classic sapajous and you'll

get your baccalaureate average !" (That's it, well said). Meanwhile,

the madness of Black Sea mutineer – aided by the butcher of

Albacete – was still well and truly visible under the thimbles.

Consequence : the corridors of my soul will bring nothing to oysters' happiness. And since *trouvères* of CAC 40 taste the analog circuits of an unmerciful destiny, I will drink all the prosthesis' fog elevated to the rank of historical monument. Then we must of course expect Maud Molyneux to react quickly and – without any pretention – that she will start comparing Gilles Deleuze to a bisexual Go(u)dot. The poor gourd and Marc Machin will then try to comb the Yves St-Laurent river... So all we have to do is scream :

"No, no, please, here it comes again !!!"

Hyperactive Oswaldo and Roberto Piazza treat Woody Woodpecker and Honest Ron Wood like dogs. That of the Baskervilles is content to bottle the wanton Harley Davidsons of the County. Here were men (Oswaldo especially) who had only been serious once in their life, and who now, at ease in their karma,

seemed delighted to climb the steps leading to Skylessness.

Artemis, feeling the chocolate melt then, gripped tightly to a silly

mushroom, soft from knee and ugly as a louse. Does their sad fate

still make you envious, eh Liberace and Walter Gropius ? It's up to

you, but the fact remains that a country priest who

also threw his meatus into nettles, everyone – including me – left in

a mad rage. Especially since we had noticed something about Saint

Christopher – the singer & journalist D. Bevilacqua, ex-Barber of

Seville... Intoxicated by rum, he had seized a windsurf board ironed

upside down – which happened to be that of his best

friend's distressed wife ! To top it all off, Michelangelo had started

climbing an apple – in the arms of this very cherry from

banky Groupe-à-Mama (Béa Tékielski).

Intermezzo 1

The wolf, the human hat and the shattered; all the words that jump out at

me (like filings on the magnet); the obscure passer-by; the moons and their

honey, stick insects and the stabbers; a load-bearing wall on the

administrative mille-feuilles*; a sea of sarcasm and the cow in flames; my*

incarnate Siamese uncle; a calf's head turtle and the Cheshire Cat (her

smile remains there, lonely); a sweet-sweet blitzkrieg & debonair

intolerance; Arthur H. and your sticky Didier Raoul(t) Volfoni; those mists

on the mane of wrinkled stool; an egg on horseback that goes humble amble

(both are cooked); the beautiful doors that slam on grateful dead ones;

two song of the glaziers; the head elsewhere and one foot in the habit; soft

human linen; two bunkers in the taxi with unpaid bills (we see

flies with receding chins)...

Chapter II

The beauty of soups will last if any toad

teems with binary elements

There you go, neither one nor two : irritated, the cherry, a mule,

the apple and a dolphin who was passing by then decided to form a

couple (!) to – all together – pull and then go up the suspenders of

one of twenty seven conspiratorial movers who rushed to the

rescue… All this happened in Guadalajara, a long time ago

(February or March 1937 ? – well, check it out).

My fine neighbor ? His authoritarian sweetheart transformed it into

picking olives, with the flick of a 'Tradition' baguette (the one at 1

euro 25). So I protest once more… Although… I know very well

that it is never easy to distinguish greens from blacks, especially when they are all on their knees ! Nevertheless, it is confirmed : a

modern-day Bluebeard is looking for a furnished apartment with a

view of a charlatan of the worst kind, *por ejemplo* my wife's

puppeteer. And if he finds one, we will be irremediably and forever

transformed into badly unscrewed puppets... So no more mysteries

as to who is pulling strings and managing the watermelons.

As a result, everything is clear again : famous fashion designers full

of themselves will point the tip of their noses. And inevitably,

sleeping with Pinocchio & Harry Truman will not only leave

sawdust all over the place : the four-poster bed will also prove to be

too hard and very unfriendly ! From then on, dear Gonzalo, all you

have to do is go and clear your mind – these ideas which are, almost

all of them, only squads of hungry snails.

Once you've been sewn, imagine a world without gods, without icons and without rabbits from mysterious Ys... Then you'll surely see the hot water bottle full of cherry pits, the one that made an idle story machine a bestseller. As soon as my ship has landed on a grape seed – a few hundred billion thousand years ago – I will marry a chair; *et para siempre* Sid Vicious and Jean Lecanuet will be the best friends in the world... So, you all – clones of Karl Schmidt-Rottluff with straps ? –, you might now see that life can be beautiful near Issoudun. Admittedly, I will be objected that the inert rain in diapers has written "Charming lol" all over the place… But from there to cooking Woody Guthrie and sipping eighteen cognacs alone... Because of – thanks to – you perhaps ?!?

In order to make birds laugh, raspberries *à la* Roger & Alan Moore snort against the pretty Angelina Merkel (the one who strives to answer questions that no one asks). The delicious phantasms of the past often coming to stupefy us with sentences, will they finally decide to go see one of my neighbors upstairs, for example the one who has scarified himself (or sacrificed ?). Well, anyway a controverted smooth talker in his spare time, Captain Cap – provided his companion had finished his internship at *Pôle Emploi* – then sent a message to a sacred cow, the very one who, amorphous, eyed the seven plagues of Egypt (phew !). We are of course talking about Jonathann – THE Jonathann who swore it on his heart and who gave beautiful rehash works to all those who would remain unworthy of the passing gadfly. That same Jon. David and so on. who, in order to stand on his own two feet and in hope of winning the lottery, one day admitted having addressed a few buxom ballerinas as you... "No need to slyly cry now !''

24

shouted popular wisdom of Gray-la-Ville. The ripped-pocketed

actress then pulled out of her hat an exquisite barn and your

enlarged shadow. Beware or rejoice in it, the fact is that it happened

on that same street, at an angle – with David Hockney *sur glace*.

Madam Fairy, this recurring dream comes back to me, but which

always leaves me dirty : a hairy Nouredine Morano wiggles her

buttocks... And, decapitated, former convicts laugh at her (It must

be said that I, a simple window cleaner, had never been able to bear

them, her and her brother…). But wait, wait, the worst thing is that

afterwards, when I wake up, I do them sweet eyes ! Both !!!

Tripping over the carpet, the inconstant wood then compresses Jack

Lang, who is crying out for help, wrapped in a sack of rice... A sack

of rice that we will find later on the back of Christine Ockrent's

handsome old faraud lover. During this time, the winded sovereign and the grotesque gas stove shoot fifteen Judith Therpauve (with a

look) and a single Francisco Ferrer (for real) – thus decoding the

extra-terrestrial guinea piggy of Montjuïc. As for Mathieu

Valbuena's little bike, he alone can beat the gums of an Azeri

Vladimir Jankélévitch; while a driver of Romanian

origin gets into his tank and begins a merciless struggle with peace.

Finally, in all this beautiful little world we will recognize Luigi

Pirandello and an uncertain Pio Marmaï, a toddler certainly

Kafkaesque as hell – but also very pleasant (saddest thing of all).

And from then on, the verdict will fall, harsh : "Poor redundant

mutt, you can't do anything more about it,

except... acquiesce to the 4-4-2 of a purplish god !"

Intermezzo 2

... twilight falling on sighing bones; the headlong rush (where there is no

longer any sun); John Lydon handsome, rotten and crucified; three chabalas

and seven roucoulettes *forever removed from the knife; auburn haired left-*

handed heaven; your enamel diamonds and some bullfighters; a few dusty

ladybugs and my soul parked on the sidewalk; the gastric reflux of Joseph

Darnand and Francis Bout-de-l'An; diverging stars in the haunted house; in

Faya-Largeau, past and its black eye; the impossible horse and the

Byzantine weasel; electric cheese in the University of errors; some lower

sea that saw me come solo with God; the mask of etic syllogisms; a glass-

toothed wolf; the plum, the orange and the box of matches

(Arnold L. knows about it); illogical starved letters...

Chapter III

You have to stretch the cursed bow, face

down on a moral window

Cold wolves get shameful loneliness. And what about clergymen

and the cousin with the worm-eaten tibia, that of the bar-tobacconist

where Andy Warhol(a) prays... Consulting

her crystal ball, Madame Z. saw me flirting with Serge Lama's

Dalaï. His starry wives, taken aback by all mania, then got on their

suitcases – and Madame Simone du Bavoir drove off !

Admittedly, the latter fished, given that piece of yak on her chin...

Nose-less : Tequila Sunrise *para* everybody ! But yes yes indeed,

that's true, all those pink flamingos adorning the socks exhibited in the port of Amsterdam are likely to frighten hairy seagulls... But

hey, they will always prefer uniforms to horn captains veterans.

Conclusion : here it is, Internet is starting

to break them again... And I'm going to abandon my sister and

Robert Le Vigan (but no, not Delphine pleeeeaaase). In the

meantime, the maths teacher, the one with beautiful ungrateful

sharks, faces and calls Nestor Burma a fat *pignouf*. Could it be

because Otto Klemperer and Ringo Starr indicted

the tiny naked gecko female ?...

Night at the musette ball : Sandrine Kiberlain nervously

caresses an annoyed jar who has tripped over the piercing carpet.

By Odin, Thor and Allah, that's the work of a small-footed

fakir ! A clean coward on (and under) him had fun fighting the

hydra of reassuring insurers & the shepherdess, stubbornly

supported by a pretty skinny mule (by the verb… and on an ugly

stepladder). She made one of the conclave's participants

decree that they had better go play on the pontoon of souls... Well

done, Marlene ! In any case, before getting married, our fiancé will

inevitably have to stuff thirteen look-alikes of Elton Jones and Brian

John – but more slender. Then, finally doing what pleases him, he

will be able to go into raptures over the

catalog of dear Malik's Rout...

In short, in the nearer future than we think, people with little means

will drink reasonable rain... Especially Mireille & Daniel

Darc (who, by the way, are often on board of the Orient-Express).

Big fans of the coming summer but a little saddened by five sparse

USB cables here and there, here come noodles of the unfaithful rapper (the very one who frankly breaks them for us)... From

autumn to spring, they trim hedges with his wife's

grandmother – the old woman who knitted scarves during half-

times of certain bass solos. However, in some remote areas, we had

shouted "Neither God nor master" to Alexander the 1st.

As expected and because the three dots tattooed on our knuckles

ordered wolves never to separate again (unless they met three

buzzards accountable for their seven errors), Joseph

Joanovici and Sister Smile, not seeing anything coming , began to

grope – in view of the pig who has just learned that he is not father

of everything. Jesus C. – as a symbol of his kindness and his

incompetence – gave them unconditional support.

The hot air coming from South leaves the police station to pay

empty deposit – the one that must deliver the whole top of a Breton lighthouse... And we are positive now : it is well over of this world

without dogmas to which we aspired. Here's

the story : a very tipsy Panchen Lama was seen yesterday, in his

simplest braces, nineteen cows laying eggs (there, very close) on a

chipped pack of Cristaline water... Yes, the buttocks

are stubborn, Mrs. Nathalie St-Cricq. And *todos los* Balkany think

no less ! Patrick Topaloff beats Ben Hur on the post, "fingers in the

nose" he still boasts... Consequences : Ei(se)nstein

and Nicéphore Niepce take the opportunity to hug Johnny Rotten –

who does not lead wide. And a pitiful Louise de Vilmorin covers

the anonymous alcoholic with kisses, in order to repay all his

Russian loans. These same borrowings that all walk with a

determined step towards a Friedrich Nietzsche-esque buffoonery

(his inflatable mustache and his false martial

air no longer deceiving anyone).

"The best way to achieve your goals is to stay straight, straight

and proud of your cuts"... "*Natürlich*, just like a nice Navajo

restaurateur can easily use everything, stuck under hoods of a sedan

chair" replies our *menu* (i.e. : skinny) philopath. Well,

you have to see... The other went on : "If you only knew, Stanislas,

how tired I sometimes feel, a bit like a landscape artist who feels as

if he's wasting away... Hearing the chords of seventh

diminished by false kings every evening from Poland – not to

mention all those other hiccups I spare you. For example, a

rehashed solo by Mark D. S. Choufleur – but not only !"...

When you also realise that Sidonie drives a car with firm hips, her

blue quince sniffing – from top to bottom – the frightened moon...

And that in the white paradise any fireproof duck wears an

attractive pig tail !!! "Why, then ?" laments in turn

Elysée's pythia… So, our president declares *in petto* :

"Because Mr. Van de Graaff's – no 'r' and 2 'f' please ! – purple

generator travels at night. And on top of that with the

ex-mother of this giant guy : Peter Hammill''

Intermezzo 3

... a Greek tragedy that would fit in four thimbles; the spirit that scratches

worms, makes me go to bed in London and then wake up in Asia; dip an

abstract rusk into the hole of its tea; one deep cave; the grace of helms and

that of the governor; a Polish dawn (Caryl Chessman sniffed the air and led

the parade); the golden claws of your eyelashes, and that particular

counter-finesse of vanity; verbal jousts that wipe out reality; a windshield

farther away now; the vegetarian satanist skinning his dog; a postman

falling asleep in the blue Ford Mustang; haughty fly; a passive vampire

fascinated by the "Shitness of Things"; wheat raising its head

and Napoleon lowering his...

Chapter IV

Waiting for the sun at the gates of a dusty

dusk (in Grantchester meadows)

A clever sailor out of ideas was worried about five Moldavian

peripatetic girls. Inch by inch, he gnawed his skins (dead following

a damage of the bones). And all that to be able to offer them, within

fifteen years, an old-timer to whom we no longer obey... Then,

suddenly, seeing a maid arriving on his bar of soap, the new animal

expectorated then belched loudly. What do you want, this one had

never been able to help but land on the tarmac of existence...

Simone Veil – instead of consulting a lawyer – then bottled Joan of

Arc and Romain. All because she (Simone or Jeanne ?) practiced naturism with Christophe Alévêque and… Simone Weil – yes

very one who always overshadowed her !

The driver who has fleas cuddles Clark Gable in the hope of

winning at Lotto's – he's a useful idiot who does his best to dance

the rumba of tender love. Three thousand policemen – Gentlemen

Clean of indefinable color – nestle them *paninis*, seedy worms and

tasselled shoes (too elaborate to be honest). They are the first of the

rope, those who run off on a *scrogneugneu* Alain Finkielkraut. In

the meantime, Djemila sent our post flying towards afterlife –

which could make up for the original blunder. And most of those

who have walked through the looking glass will tell you that – will

tell ??? – : you will now have to scan tons of kraft paper (yes, the

one that makes you mope). But happily, there will still and always

be some new.radical.solutions/ghosts – in brown shirts... In return

– under the lime trees –, we will always be able to continue to

apprehend life, all together… Uh, well – that's the price to pay.

The excess of bay leaf in steaks is excellent for startling cooks at

Le Bourget. Because, by treating these unfortunates with warts, we

will very quickly be able to prove that grandfather and his poultices

are not the cause of STD's that overwhelm my seraph. Well done

for him since he only lives on plunder. At the same time,

Marguerite (Victor ?... No, there are two 't''s !) tries to kidnap

Olivia Ruiz, Knut Hamsun & Gayelord Hauser for the personal

consumption of their famous gruff sailor. With the same perspective

as usual routine, that is to say : a purist orange that beats the

triumphant hippopotamus to snow (the one who drinks

infinity instead of consulting a shrink)… In other terms, it's a bit of

a shame for Slade and Caesar salad's lovers.

Kiki de Montparnasse and Bibi-la-Purée have run out of everything, they are patching up rhythmic beetles as best as they can… So has he time to put on a green tweed pullover ? Well if that's the case, I will gladly denounce you at 1, place des Petits-Pères !!!!! As always and forever, the penultimate of Mohicans – clean on him like the northern districts of Marseille – will then call a hypothetical sieve. And, however, bringing strictly nothing to investigation, the master of Greater Paris site will invite him to come and debate on all the channels of Vincent Bolloré's moron group... Well, it's always been like that, so : ok for me.

While taking a shower, Coco Suaudeau's FC Nantes is still arguing with the Ace of Spades – remember Lemmy ? The two would so love to spend a night with Sophie and *le Mime Marceau*… And with the Papin sisters, these perpetually angry &

anonymous guinea fowls. The hesitant bat, one who loved an umbrella, finally opted for the said Jean-Pierre Papin – an ex-dancer *à la* Marius Petipa – and for thirteen stories that lead to nothing (not even to good grains of drunkenness). Listen to her now, we can see that she never ironed or downed her clumsy kid's gin ! The latter, all alone in a room, had once caught a glimpse of a fuzzy shape half man half devil – Paul on skis ? Cabu ?? –, which form 1) had quickly ordered him to exhibit – in front of everyone – the crumbs of cake scattered on a plaintive carpet, and 2) had launched him with bronze and threatening : "Au revoââââârrr".

On board of his Vélib', Saint-Ex' loved getting a manicure from the needy Blue Sandinista… Yet their room was not cleaned ! And in addition he was paid just above the minimum wage... Therefore let's be serious : television can now only be watched in replay, at

Vel' d'Hiv' or elsewhere. Perhaps later – one vile morning of nail

clippings – she will come to announce her departure. And then, as I

never realized that the sea and my mother are Kabyle accountant

subjects (to the law of kidneys), your worst friends – :

Justine L, a warmy G. C. Lichtenberg and Fidel Castro the

Trump(eter) – will finally be able to overtake the city

of Ur strolling in pastures.

(Well, do you really believe that – do you ??)

Intermezzo 4

... the jam of crimes; a concrete couscous pot; the moon that makes you

think about electric Camemberts; Charles Meryon and Amedy Coulibaly

fleeing everywhere; the well-meaning idiot; six hundred eyes wide open on

nothingness; testicles of Boulevard Magenta (they rest in peace); Thaïs

d'Escufon married to Erika Zemmour; poissard *philosophers and the*

shameless tortoise; an orchestra of things; the skirt full of eyelids; a Spanish

worm at the old people's fair; three psychorigid corpses; a rhinoceros and

forty two large hearths (my brothers in thickness); many nervous vacuum

cleaners (themselves nephews of a white spouse); a benevolent Nazi (he

hangs out behind the scenes of life); seven Afghani half-smiles

under a beautiful killer's trench coat (your sister is there,

very close to verandas)...

Chapter V

Since it rains dwarfs on Ramatuelle I wake up in my dreams (6060842)

Naked as a worm under his Perfecto, Frank N. Furter thinks that nothing beats a little jam on the wedding dresses of Gaston d'Orléans. Playful, he will end up accusing Claude Guéant – the poor man is in full questioning and no longer has much health (well, so to speak)... As for the Lappish rabbit, he will push a small volcano into the void then put inside tear-filled juice – and his latest Nike sneakers. Go ahead and don't worry, beautiful horsewoman with a blunt soul, the mother of fishes often makes them ties and other pie shovel collars... In the end, she will go into ecstasies in front of their wagging tails – merry appendages where mantillas and retorts are invited. And the man who had the astonishing ability to

split himself will one day find himself at the desert's bottom

and on the verge of drowning. After giving birth to twenty two

pieces of music, he will amaze himself with

a simple flowerpot.

Gérard & Edouard Philip(p)e, after three journeys in space-time,

wallow there again – again and again. With relish ?... Let's

see : the Tapper of our donkeys swoons over a sandwich from

islands of the same name. Then, still lower from the front(ispiece),

it rushes on RN52… Pitiful destiny – but what delicious carnage.

On this, to make ends meet, Socrates swallows a punk, thus defying

the law of Rodin, Mœbius and Gauguin... My god Michel, it's still

Camille Claudel who will complain ! And yet, stunned by a perfect

copy of her portraits by l'abbé Sieyès, an auctioneer is still looking

46

for herself in front of the man from Serbia, the one who laughs at

everything. That's why I demand a vodka and the little blue horse

byFranz Marc, to this gourd of Carla B. (We are certainly

courageous but not reckless...) Further on, a golden family is grafted

with anger, and a somewhat milky Ivan Lendl casts a nostalgic look

at the Four Bearded Men, all dressed to the nines (except Fred

Mella and Omar Scie). As for daddy – still not having finished

sleeping off his wine – he should mount two old horses on the way

back and wrap, with great care, seven grimoires with yellowed

pages. And to finish, it will also be necessary

to put you in danger, my cabbage !

Marie-Thérèse Urdillo (?-1778) and G. Bernanos broke all the

tender phalluses. It must be said that a live legume from the Persian

Gulf stood by their side, in simple Eve attire. But the tequila without Google – drool and glue obscured by the clouds – had also

brought an attractive Tonton Macoute to heel... It's still

Vauvenargues' fault : as usual, he's trying his best to bribe Brett,

Laurent & Anne Sinclair. The *Gilets Jaunes* Freddy Krieger and

Robby Krueger, they show themselves without any shame –

supported as they are by a Simone Signoret-Kaminker wearing a

gold but semi-remarkable helmet. As for Cap'tain Igloo, he always

seems a bit silly to us/you, decked out in his chapka. It must be said

that stories of succubus had always made him shudder – without

however having ever let a single revolutionary fop pass through

him !! *Al dente*, they nevertheless continue to swell certain

communard ankles, those of cowards who have gone over to

communitarianism (for instance R. Rigault or Adolphe Thiers,

but not Eugène Pottier nor C. Delescluze).

48

Soulless Packing Grand Parade meets the Moon-Lighting Knight

(in Bath, Surrey). Result : rhythm cockroaches and a music box

violently criticize the nuns of Liverpool – whatever their shameful

manager thinks. Suddenly, Josiane Balasko took banjo lessons

overnight. Then the Thin Dark Duke – in fact David Jones laughing

out loud – started shooting an out-of-control Baruch (von) Spinoza

because he was at his wit's end (his affair with Heraclitus had just

ended). That was to be expected, but still... In short and to resume, a

frog basking on its favorite jack had snorted energetically and

sprayed two Waffen-SS's who were passing by. She (the feminine

frog) was in fact counting (on) her flock but unfortunately we could

finally see, in the distance, a romantic *tête-a-tête* – one of which a

little giant had involuntarily become hero (a

hero indeed indebted for everything).

The old yellow vest-shirt of the cyclist with cross-eyed gaze

scatters my beautiful chubby Christmas tree – to the four winds. As

for Portugueses, feeling guilty as the centenary of Badajoz's

conquest approaches, they eat less and less. And because of all

those pretty thatched roofs, Julian Cope sues Martin Hirsch (and

Canon Kir). However, we have since known that, from the top of

his micro-perch, he struts about – naked, in rhythm… And the worst

part is that all of this is perfectly justified ! But beware, epilogue :

this antique jewel that Romane B. liked so much was actually lying

on an aquiline ball bed, a block of ice between legs and over head.

He twisted, in his baleful eyes, a poet in love with a nervous star...

And so, final conclusion : this is indeed a tribute to all

ruminants who want to kill us (i.e. Marcel Bascoulard, Ernst

Ludwig Kirchner and Lord Kitchener).

50

Intermezzo 5

... the techno-vagina and a libertarian clitoris; a hasty accountant scrapped

on three offshore wind turbines (one of which belonged to Dr. Petiot); putrid

shells, the Blessed Virgin, Dada and your clergyman; a cloud married to his

pants; deep chocolates served with an enchanting toast; livers and all types

of life (the weak vulva wants them); those nurseries and the machine-gunned

locomotive; your smoky talk about the clothesline (A. Layne is not fooled);

false night on the right; a mutinous Chinese with his twenty-two potato

mashers; Simon the Magician, mad girl Gigi plus Charlie the Surineur *in the*

shade of a blue scoundrel; the paraphernalia of

women who inhabit a child...

Chapter VI

Coughing up clouds under a pergola in flames can make laugh violet

Bobby Ewing puffs out his chest and, ethereal under his bomber jacket, sniffs the wall. However, make no mistake about it : he is jealous of the limp gorilla who makes Inspector Gadget scream with pleasure. In Savannah's savannah, an elephant with ridiculously tiny ears had nevertheless left for a day of rat race, hoping to catch up with my club sandwiches and a sterile eel. And even – via condiments – controlling the Mater Dolorosa of confinement, namely : Karine Lacombe, Ian Curtis, Pierre & Gilles (from Genoa), Ivan Rioufol, Jimmy Page/Dean… and Marion Maréchal-Nous-Voilà. Otherwise apart from that, each misery and/or (well) received idea constitute a tributary or a confluence of my superb

river logic… "And why thaaaaaaaaaaaaaaaaaaaaaat ? " asks the

minstrel in the gallery (Jacques Derrida to tell the truth). Well,

because as long as beauty of soup lasts, a toad is teeming with

binary elements. And because a tiny assassin, gone to buy

cigarettes, had not returned (the prospect of yet another new world

order, who knows ?). It must be said that outside his home he had a

guilty relationship with M. McLuhan and his Fender Telecasters

(recently, he shaved all their eyebrows)... Well then, answer me, all

of you poor Keith Richards : did you finally straighten it out ?!?

Marcel Proust and Tito Puente, sweating like in Russian novels,

have shared accommodation with some kind of cacochyme guy's

racist snout… ¡ *Por fin !* Neither one nor two, and without

consulting any instructions, Iggy Pop & James N. Österberg run away to Karcher boundaries and a dilapidated mouse vomiting

seventeen morbid Groucho Marx (Harco and Chipo being out for a

while). Even more: at Amédée Cousin St. (n° 3), it oozes leap doves

escaped from the sky and from deadly *vinasse*. So, since then,

autumn's dust and animist laments think about astral nightingales.

So sad ! Other things : those who know the joys of stationary travel

will save themselves a lot of expense by drooling over them, in their

thoughts and from islands to isthmuses… Or : let them raise two

Bresse chickens with all our strength, if possible with the help of a

honeyed Geronimo and his memories. Oh yes, also note that –

known as the Afghan cardinal's white wolf – my uncle, a famous

handyman, can no longer help giving Isabelle Balkany and Betty

Page a makeover… And not even your future offspring.

Virtuous *poussahs* are displayed at the Macumba. Such a waste...

Because long before, comatose or not, they could have taught the

millennial history of Tonkin with silky apples. Be that as it may,

false twins who still believe in fairy tales are donning their finery

tools... They are waiting for six little chimney sweeps that – be

careful ! – won't want to die before having known the deleterious

fragrances of SNCF. A little further, on the Cambridge side, Lucifer

Sam having shared a roommate with Syd-le-Barré(tt), red rain

appeared out of nowhere and devoured St-Thomas (with disgust).

Why, then ? Well, because "Republic is myseeeeellfff !"

– and not him, nor all others

(as for the beginning : copyright from J.-L. M.)

On Eddie Cochran's scarf, a slimy lobster (and its precise

gestures) compromise(s) my future and defile(s) my chakras for all eternity... Above all, don't try to lick snow under the blue flashing

lights, that would make you smile and give food for thoughts !

Because yes, I admit it : I often simulate with Jacques Doriot and

Johan Neeskens. That said, in my defense – ahem, if I may say so...

– the first is in fact only a fickle road-mender, who gave birth to

bundles of creatures foreign to the Germanopratine bovine race...

This is what brought us all down – here, elsewhere and at the *Fête à*

Neu-Neu. Because Mr. Zeus de Rocancourt came out at supper and,

taking his reverse bath, he talked about it to Laetitia Castafiore, the

nerd who kills many old plows. And so, all the same : how on earth

do you want to expect byzantine asteroids of motley planets to

survive so easily – after such an existential gout attack ?!?

Intermezzo 6

... a tadpole's duplicity; the asian Bernard Lacombe updated by the

franchouillard *Lacombe Lucien (it was all written); to make quickly the*

crane foot at the foot of a crane; clumsy shadows under certain sharp

plants; the last man, death in soul; lost items; eyes that pour into the void;

the relief of people of stars, and bloody dummies; this past which bellows

like a limp ox; love on this scaffolding; a blaze of cinders on old

eiderdowns; all the fights in nightgowns (SOS, God barks, we have to open

the door for him !); the eternal drool and an assiduous practice of ski

jumping; shuttle between skies and the gutters of Oscar; the angry

umbrella on an operating table; the deceptive appearance of all your

mirrors; three mathematicians shaken by their gases; Carla Bruni and

Gérard Labrunie, both completely strangers to themselves...

Chapter VII
Young old men and old children
swallowing rainy resentment
(Detergents of soul)

One fine Saturn morning, I forgot everything about me – then

found myself with this pretty unicorn who had come

to push my collar around... As if you can't accuse a pack of holy

water without major risk ! Now, dancing the most beautiful

tangos in the world, I also managed to scan my husband for a

moment. This man who seemed likeable at first sight, did

you really think that he was going to take charge of the

accounts ?... No, and you have been warned : some are no longer

obliged to go into exile – on the hunt for *Indigo Revers*. Anyway, the smallest of Grand Orient's masters has since invited additional

information (which no longer brings anything new).

It's always the same story – since Adam the Spoiler,

Eve and the coming of *PlayStation*...

And above all, no one is now more eager for Margot to undo her

bodice. Because the rotten user manual files a complaint against

Gustave Flaubert, among other things for nocturnal noise (but not

only) – and this in order to overcome his fear of flying.

Anyway, let's quickly come back to the purple hen

which was chosen by Guerlain house to embody Papa Smurf's

singing (Papa Smurf is that pal from the Andalusian village

lost in the Sierra). It turns out that (s)he is angry with

me… So what, does that mean anything to you either ?! Rocambole,

he, all grumbling, will inevitably revolt, again and against

Rock'n'roll (he stands on a bizarre piece of furniture). As for

James Caan, driven by demons of sophism, he will feel the need to

be a perfect trickster (in all areas and senses of possible).

Resultado : as arduous as the task may be, they

will innovate and dare to create works which will impress us

all – Lark-on-the-take and Postman Cheval included.

Meanwhile, unreally diaphanous, a quivering bulldog cajoles the

profiler who never misses fearless targets. And suddenly he

exchanges his best shirt – the one he wore every sunday while

dreaming – for a honeymoon (superb indeed, but still a little

off the mark). Hidden under a bell jar, the abstruse dog

of 'La Grange' – *AtoZ Top* is his father – throws boiling oil on

dynamic infinity. My god, how beautiful ! Then, while he thought that no more hope would be allowed to them, a forgotten singer sent

a declaration of fiery hatred to this extraordinary

sunset which each evening filled

our hearts with bitterness. Since then, we've been walking down

the street singing, a red flag in our pockets –

cos' it's much prettier that way.

A Mongolian heating engineer has put love up against the wall

without anyone being able to intervene. His double (Joseph

Goebbels in drag queen) shoots a Merovingian commercial for

Valéry Giscard D'Estiny – yes the one you can still meet,

silly, at the Luxor Bar. It's without any particular motivation that,

from wednesday to friday, an executive secretary spotted – coiled

up in the shelter of a grove – three hundred and twenty

liters of red wine. In order to forget that his wife ran away with his

best enemy, she waves her little paws

in all directions. In fact, this former chartered accountant –

cheating certainly, but also an attractive mobile phone – seeks to

impress the Hall of Mirrors. What more can be said ? – he's

vaticinating all time during my favorite show, spreading all his

knowledge… Well, therefore, I'm going to trample

over his roasted marshmallows at

night – the better way to philosophize and

melt away from everything !

God, polymorphous architect who runs around in cream, wears a

dull kilt. On the other hand, the lonely & eco-friendly mourners

continue to brick their 4X4's, while Alain covers Carl Jung...

And all that because of the neighbor's dog : Ousmane. This is why

Marcel Campion unconsciously sips an orangeade and beats the

boss's daughter to snow... All that to overcome his terrible fear of

beautiful immigrants from Cadiz ! As for Frida,

Jacques Brel's atomic Blonde, she raves about Marisol Touraine, a

beautiful animal murdered by the Vert Galant – one evening of May

1976 (remember Glasgow ?). What else ? Well Jean Cocteau's

twins – a fearful household cricket that everyone shamelessly

recommends eating – one day had the idea of going in exile towards

Canada – which Fifi ultimately did not dare to. In fact he & she

became taciturn melancholy dreamers, and straddle a few horizontal

hats every morning. With insolence.

64

Intermezzo 7

... the significant red sea urchin (it is sold to prawns); weird rescue kisses;

Tristan Hilar taking care of his overcoat; your vile obsession : a cat

delousing her little breeds; dad of butterflies (the one who manages to tear

his tears); the Valley of Crimson Legions (please return there); the red-

haired butcher spying on us; good conscience of cruelty; a dandy from

trenches at the turnstile of fame; the overlapping of my wrinkles; to wash

down dark chocolate and swallow bird milk; the memory of ruined boilers

(unfortunately, but hooray !); the frail Broadway

cheerleader and her restless cyanide wand; the ultimate ''not wise under

your loins''; this subtle scent of orange blossom and bitter almond (it floats

in the air); Sören Kierkegaard slumped in his wheeled bathtub (lithium

paste adorns his sad twisted ankles)...

Chapter VIII

Wherever it hides, fear of mosquitoes
excludes the equidistance of marble rivers

On a summery autumn sunday, Nature – in all its forms – was

doing its thing. - "I would need other shoes than these dividing

sandals..." - "Oh yes, and why not also invoke the contagious

madness of this chic citizen !?! ", retorted the grumpy Providence –

(nothing to say, it was perfectly seen)... In the process, Pythagoras

and his two *Reblochons* – infinity and nose in handlebars – got the

union grafted on crime in the chest. A good point for Hong-Kong

and Maitre Eckart, who watches over the shadow of his triumphant

rabbit ! Her giraffe also roams with a slightly doggy transverse

poodle. Perched on his high heels – it's always the same thing when you take nature for what it's not – the slender professor of physics

sings 'La Traviata' to him, while vigorously shaking a thick

Damoclès… Try so do something about it ! Anyway, in the end :

spasmophile though always up for *gaudriole*, the *Chartreux* of

Parma gets yellow sow in his skin (the one who was emptied by

Johannes Gutenberg, first startuper in history).

By dint of waiting for all these ungrateful mothers, I no longer

moan without conviction. And inevitably Samuel Beckett will again

and again retain his flatulence – theatrical kind of *cassoulet* –, only

to rationalize it much later... Almost a gagged undertaker who

pinches for your toes. As a result, C. Darwin will stealthily restart

an ice cream cone with two very sarcastic scoops (like for instance :

a rum-tar flavor)… Astride a washing machine, Arielle

Dombasle and JPP are already still laughing.

Now, finally alone, big nipples decided to swallow the detailed food

of adorable Ali (the one who lies). Then, sick as a dog, he managed

– with difficulty – to breathe on the doe-eyed inspector. And on the

ash RAM (that of Adam Drivers's corpse). Proof : the Manosque

sandals, the titanium ankle socks… and this dialogue : "Josépha,

when someone talks to me about *Tramontane*, I take out my

revolver's dwarves sneeze... In short, your

attitude is appalling and inadmissible; and all

you have to do is call S.P.A.. End of message" (!?!)

In Bern (Stéphane or Switzerland ?) : 24 Mormons haven't aged a

bit… Well, here it is, as I've always told you : a strange life is better

than the one of Jules Grevy. He could only sleep bent over, in a gun

bed... After all, maybe he should have been adopted

by a french *collaborateur* of the forties, a former man of honor who lives now at Passy cemetery. Who knows ?

Nevertheless, how pitiful and violent is your diaphanous aristocratic

smile !! And your horizon-blue gaze, not pretty to see… It cowardly

accuses *Le Grand Meaulnes* and its straps. And Michel Denisot

reassembles those of the Loch Ness monster passed *au karcher*.

Travelling in a TGV, they will both – the two

Michel – dance vertically.

In the past, a mythical animal gifted for nationalism had quickly

prepared the crossing of the Atlantic – a body of water recently

recovered by a caucasian circus. The mandolin then copied a

pretentious bagpipe... And finally : a fat extinct fireman stunned

Xi'an's terracotta brother. At the same time, one thousand two

hundred Laurent Wauquiez, charismatic and classy as one might wish, were preparing to assassinate chubby hunters (those who can

no longer breathe), so... So, I don't understand anything !

That said Ibrahim – and to end with this –, let's not worry : in the

end they will all admit defeat when Aline (the activist) appears –

and then will cry for him (Laurent) to come back at the

Universités d'Eté. This was to be demonstrated.

*P*lötzlich, some Ivan claims : "That puffy gas cooker grabbed an

uneasy Martin Heidegger". Possible answer : "No shame in that,

even if môôôôsssssieur should be glorified to become a delivery

driver in a Joe Dassin song..." To resume : yes, Emile Jacotey –

incredibly imaginative hostess – likes to tease and provoke four

mice fallen in his whisky. And the space Cardinet bridge has

certainly left to brag – albeit very timidly –, in fact dressed like the

late Claude Chabrol (Gabriel Fauré for his friends).

We all also intend to scratch Lydie Bastien and Alof de

Wignacourt's crusts, at the exit of motorway... Above

all, do not spread these news !

Alice and the 8 *Scaroles* covet their neighbours' plates, which

contain a childhood friend arisen by chance. So, outraged, Le

Castor de Beauvoir and Sam Peckinpah will call them all to order,

via our arrangement/law of July the 14th (29th ?), 1881. The

risk to be run will therefore be this chain reaction : foreskin

opposite and a good part of the population who hang languidly,

damn proud to be able to climb the stairs four by four (without ever

having read any kind of instructions). And in the end, a

suffocating air will foreshadow this dark finale : at last, at last,

the Games of May beginning !

Intermezzo 8

... Christ on a scooter and two fake cumulonimbus clouds (they excel in the

art of kung-fu); the impatient shadow; three gyrovague monks in the airhole

of childhood; a sober openwork bedside table; the error of having been

oneself (that is to say : brimborions *and rattle); six thousand and twenty-*

three valetudinary catechumens; my stomach that lights up a living room

(thanks to football, that billiards of the prairies); wallpaper bodies;

dromomania rising up in everyone's court; the horns of stars; a

conspiratorial mystic living off the hook of nothingness; four jovial

misanthropes and their morality; a small bicycle in

the head of two pebble-dogs...

Chapter IX

The subtle rotting movements and pretty whispers from tomorrow's snows

"**T**errible combination of blood – and that apple pie under pillows of winds !" shouted the heretical *Gauleiter*… "Certainly, certainly, but should we also post the pangs of intelligence around ties ?" – I thought to myself. "Yeah, I'll admit I dozed off a bit but now are you finally going to get everything back up to speed ?!?" Alas, I had indeed left sin but, if you have enough discernment, the plows should smell bad again – I loved so much those who had given birth to a tapeworm and four salamis... This was the applicant's last replica led by a hot seat. The tiny shoemaker who wanted to go dancing then borrowed the ulterior motives of pain. And, while he persisted in wanting to untie them, a

charming, haughty mermaid, running after his bus, ordered him to

do all the ironing and to clean his trays well. Too bad for him,

because after all : did he really believe in surviving ??

In the land of cuddly toys, sweeties are sweet and strong at the

same time : they attack indefinitely a Bruno Carette crying all the

tears of his horn. Alongside this, one handsome old man in

kangaroo underwear examines the pain of time, then gets vaccinated

against iguanas, moving sand and their lovers. However,

when in my life it was cold, a mosquito net on the back dared to

stop stepmother in shorts. For what ? Because she was

short-legged and determined to run for yet another term. With that,

a German boxer knocked out in the fifth round resigned

from his position as general manager – in order to have a little more

time to observe Lily Rose Depp (by the way, she looks a bit 'bionic',

doesn't she ?). Now he & she are gesticulating in all directions, in

the last of expensive subways... *Pour résumer*, my

advice would therefore be : come quickly (the sooner the better).

Allergic to gluten, Angela Davis rushes to Gertrude Stein.

His (?!?) problem is that a pimply teenager, HSBC client

and occasional putschist from february 1981, wants to steal all the

Nutella jars from Mandryka's family (Nikita is its flagship). A

notorious upstart although used to cleaning up other

people's homes & a senile sailor sailing against the tide still stood

there, unable to recognize their faults. And then afterwards,

he began to irritate the Horse Guards already affected by dances of

Saint-Guy... Too much indeed.

Also annoying a scenario crying out for truth, it smells of leather

and Africa. And since, in addition, I cannot assume my carbon 14

balance sheet... After all – and therefore – I demand some

indulgences, plus walls that have knocked out the prince

we are ta(l)king (ab)out. By the way, why was this one made

of this – the vile foot soldiers might think... Well because

throughout Far North, God – undressed or in

tuxedo – smells of hot sand !!!

A *fuori di clase* player had made me known to the whole world by

inventing effervescent parts of himself... Unfortunately

he had not foreseen all this ugliness ignored by pretty love & hate,

those who are tangled to Jacob's brushing – delighted norwegian

lobster Rabbi, ain't it ? "We will have to clean the gruff mother's

sink" explains mummy Dolto (F.) to F(elipe) Pétain. "So that the shooting star climbs to the top of the tree and begins a playful trip

through forests... And don't forget : take a deep breath before the

end of this Collaboration", will she also end up admitting...

So this is it, choose for Christ's sake... It will be either ninety

rockets at Machecoul, or Razibus Zouzou at

7, Champs-Aiguisés ! Or, at worst : the

Wehrmacht's tenderness on our clothesline. Which – at last

and in any case – always have led to kings

and queens of approximation (too bad indeed)...

Gros-Dada(ism) passed away. This is why Pr. Choron whips gray

cows and deep marmots – those who like to sleep with the organ-

asthma of worried cuckolds. Downright soup with milk, Anthony

Delon also attacks Audrey Hepburn, herself pursued by a bumpkin of the worst kind : it is Stanley Kubrick sinking, in full existential

questioning. Because when you draw your

literary metaphors from certain daily lives, you have to expect that

the hours will be increased by twenty-one musicians.

When in fact – after extensive investigation – it is just La

Maintenon full of aces who robs seven plates of disgust which

falled backwards. However, some followers of

transcendental medi(t)ation – we never knew why – love to walk in

scandals. Lightly dressed, close-knit people bite into

the reindeer queens of Santa Claus, in the regions accounting for

everything and nothing… Uh, did you say "Ancestral rites" ?!?

Well, you may not be wrong after all.

Intermezzo 9

... the irenic ether of the High Paternal; five beautiful sad craters; a

daughter of the bishop and the floating TIPP (it's a pretty ampersand with

iridescent tones); overconfident short scales; our noses at dusk and your

mercenary heart; the return of the large transparency; all the "Don't throw

any more, go ahead and see if you don't believe me !"; chickens on a

libertarian G-spot; loose chivalry of dogs; truth and its lies in the colors of

silk; a sweet and salty fairy; some washing machines, drunk in the passage

of time; twelve flatshares on the fly; a turntable and the sinks forever

darkened; that shepherdess from Ivry, and the man who

did the trick at Reculettes *Lane; memories of the future, ptosis*

and volapük à la *Père Ubu...*

Chapter X

The depressed shaman and his
stubborn rake

$\mathbf{A}$ bunch of racist Chinese tourists – unhappy rats who can't stop

thinking about the puffy weasel in Nanjing – jump with both feet on

a sheepish (but enchanted all the same) Jeffrey Lee Pierce.

Intending to land at Mobutu Sese Seko'and the Prince of morbidity,

Louis la Brocante then goes out of his beaten track and begins to

sustain himself, thus weaning Pascal – Blaise (Ok, ok, this was just

for fun). Meanwhile, the priest's cat and the prettiest

Imam had discovered Lascaux's cave, while they were following

the advice of an irritated hedgehog (each one had been invited to his

cellar). As for Ulysses & Alice, they both fell in love with the Ascaso Brothers, who nevertheless soiled the milk with their

excretions… "Spiss' di counasse, you lose nothing

by waiting ! " they said then, in unison and straight away. Along

sad Saint-Martin Canal, imperturbable, Philippe Katerine continued

to have strange sources of inspiration : 1) Cousteau, 2) his red cap,

3) a grouch and 4) two diving suits ("And his darling brother

Pierre-Antoine, uh then ?!", one might ask…).

The blue swedish sun of Claire Brétécher pulls up straps of three

Jaffa oranges, and then suddenly laughs as she watches Michel

Onfray pass by in the flat green country of Candy... Better that than

nothing else. Because the fact is that, one day of 1624, Count

Bert(h)old Brecht had nervously caressed clones of Karl Marx and

Carlos Castaneda still in their pajamas – in the shower. They were

both lit by a libidinous looking silly lamp. We then heard

in the distance : "Sooooo, Yannick Noah thinks nothing beats

Prince of Darkness, uh ?!?" There you go, we told you

once, and   it's confirmed : the French right is,

forever and ever, the dumbest in the world. So certainly :

"Nénesse-City makes law", we will say to ourselves... However,

columns of refugees on the (winding) Malaga/Almeria road,

were they just a simple trip to a disco ??!!?? After all, there must

have been leaks – yes, and the suitable rabbit

is for sure transgender.

In this sentimental vaudeville where doors slam, a man who had

the ability (innate DNA acquired) to split *lui-même*,

one day found himself locked in the kitchen (at the end of corridors,

right after the desert). We have since grown tired of him… Kind of result : now each and every one can no longer shrink from all these

lovers who are reinventing themselves… For their

defense, we must say that the fashion for unicorns – used for

everything and anything – had often constituted a terrible lack of

taste. Whereas from the start, when you hear a pin drop

at a party, all you have to do is kneel and worship

Rodrigo de Triana Street.

In any case what is certain is that Mr. Coquelin-Cadet's

toad and an azure blue chief warrant officer hitchhike a pair of

reasonable buttocks (yet born from the penultimate rain). And

seeing that Zabou Breitman hides a bottle under her

bed (the one that speaks like Raymond Barre), taxis spotted in her

face immediately, intenting to kidnap them. Both at the same time.

86

Tired of the antics from a radio host, D'Artagnan sent his prostate waltzing towards the great beyond – precisely here, at the very place where a tight Djinn was flirting with a mimosa-scented whistleblower… "Yes, my suspenders are all iridescent – so where's the problem ?? he argued breathlessly.

These virtual violinists, filling glasses of their guests, were helped in this by a not-so-smart little trickster. And that was their loss : during this time musky rodents in a state of decomposition had taken self-defense lessons, very close to the bouquet of Lilywhite Lily in the Valley of the Dolls... And Voltaire, quite skinny, saved a very cute Jean Ziegler from drowning, and 19 empty coconuts !

It happened by the river of bitter tears – and everything that comes with it.

Performing a lover of the French language and no longer knowing

whom to worship, 49 aliens finally rallied a brand new Sufi

underling. Drunk to the marrow, some of them then decided to

immolate themselves under two wheels (and a half) of a double-

decker bus. (By the way, a tibetian gentle hypocrite was also there

that night, looking for two self-hypnotified serpentine charmers…)

As for many Elvis Presley fans, they continue to stalk promotions.

And sales reps manage to sell seven dwarfs and their tasselled

knives… But also all my post-it decorations – which had been

deliberately thrown into oblivion. Publishing her diary on the web, a

teenager (illegitimate son of Vince Taylor and "Pr." Didier Raoult)

brought to her mother a pot of butter – and the 666

horrible death masks of a pharaoh cyclist. Ultimately, on arrival, as

planned : Syd V and Hanna Schygulla become Denise F, while

Héloïse melts in Gaston G… Good enough, but on the other hand,

how can we – after all this – confuse a bearded woman with Mrs.

Alliot-Marie ?!? And wouldn't a nun in need of children have taken

all possible steps to be able to adopt eight muses of (one of) the

Boko Haram's fifty anthills, eh ?? Anyway, for that she

could quite simply have claimed :

a) the most irreproachable mental hygiene,

b) your shining inverted pyramids, and

c) Sun studios in Memphis...

Yours for said.

Intermezzo 10

... the reflection of four puddles, which made me fall in the sky; any

afterlife; two swallowers of Light passing through the box at Gand, Belgium

(via blue chimneys); nights of faceless eyes; the impasse of fear, the one that

gives onto silent avenues; lilies in the vestibule (which make me bathe in my

watch); the world in a kiss; a fatal squash in Grenoble, with the last of the

Trastamares; life, in consideration of your evanescent taxpayer; all that and

nothing at the same time (sustainable to brigands of thought); P. Praud, that

useful idiot with the well trimmed beard; coral stools; your mouths in ruins

under poor tunics; fully great murderous aids; the passing oysters

and their small estrémègne men; the very last lift of swaying rhythms;

Raphaël Quenard and Pio Marmaï playing Yannick;

M. Perebenesiuk's beautiful frozen suns & 17 salty rabbi(t)s...

Chapter XI

*Soldiers, the Piper and a pot of
sorrows at potron-minet
(Had this dream stopped ?)*

"The apocalyptic gurus at Ikea, they should be sprayed with

syndromes... Let them go back to spend their BEPC in the lakeside

city, these Minou Drouet of the climate !" - "Ok, no need to argue

anymore, anyway we will always find catacombs of wisdom at the

Saint-Arnoult tollbooth..." On top of that, the pretty mixed-race

ugly woman (Anna, the worst piranha) filed a complaint

against slumped strangers from the North-Express – for night

noising. Poor thing, it was just Michel Houellebecq at the Musette

ball… So a pot-bellied shy Garcimore hitchhiked

Errico Malatesta, his long teeth flirting

with the orange Grand Vizier (who, via phylloxera and mildew, was spreading his gall on tiny ice packs – with passion).

While dreaming of a less spatial existence, General Yagüe (remember Badajoz ?) lost his pants and found himself in a state of extreme weightlessness, hovering above the plays. On *Gran Via* then appeared the Snow Queen – she had been born this very morning and was already passionately kissing a drunk (but) dead car. The latter had already sketched out eight outlines of her project, flabbergasted to note that her writings came out doomed, all at once. It must be said that she had studied 'The Mermaid of Mississippi' for a long time... "Here's enough to complete a trilogy on a diving board – with the timid neighbor upstairs" she says to herself. Left behind, cavities of Beaumont-sur-Oise will soon be able to blow on the embers of malaise. This is a risk we all have to

take... Fortunately, at half-time, a grumpy touch and

its desalinated lasso will solve the solved

problems (nothing more than that).

"**A**ll the Bavarian skin pants should climb a dog !", shouts some

grunchy teenager to the Japanese ambassador (cos' we are stuck

between two stations ?). An old man, careful not to

make reappear the basic instincts of EHPAD's supervisors, knocked

over his plate of Bolognese pies (via the rant of CanalPlus

subscribers). So let's protect what is beautiful about it – and also the

aggressiveness with which its litron expresses itself ! Meanwhile, a

boring pink ear has got a bowl transplanted into her; and

since then she has gone to cut her teeth with (and against) 37

anxious Charles Louis de Secondat (yes, yes, Montesquieu).

So, in the end, meta-theories that are not always very inspired stay

there, dressed like aces of spades… Because their

cats – which have gasified – will never come back to them. They

were all pale blue, similar to African skies – yes, those of that

good Saint Eloi, our pal who invented everything by

the school of crime.

Because a great (but a bit tart) coat rack keeps on dealing his bread

with John Lenin & Paul McCarthy, Louis XIV the pimp curls up

against stupid guardians of half-sleep. A Red Sea dog steps then

on La Pasionaria (Pilar Franco's rival). Plus, instead of consulting a

good shrink – 'Sibeth Ndiaye the Rogue' for example – they

compose a song together, about a synthetic thug. According to the

hemiplegic turtles of anarchist lesbians, islamist diggers

and followers of the Throne Fair would not be Macron-compatible.

94

My favorite books therefore find it difficult to submit to authority,

denouncing the weak candidates of Eurovision and 4 incompetences

of their six wives. All this to say that the balance sheet

of Carbone and Spirito is not

so bad – especially in PACA region (but not only)… And once

again : another defeat for Eugène Saccomano

and his literary claims.

The lesson givers – who themselves have a lot to learn on the

meanders leading to Alcazar fortress – should understand that their

attitude engenders the desire to think with their feet. Must

they be stupid, these pedants of our glorious Fifth Column ! In

addition, a specter with amoebas, helped by nutcracker vampires,

weaves tenuous ties with Haute-Vienne's sub-prefecture...

And all that gives the spice market – or three thousand liters of happiness – equivalent to a strong gaze. Afterwards, a gas station

attendant at the end of his rights eats all members of *Les*

Compagnons de la Chanson. And – unexpected catastrophe ! – Jack

Nicholson and his libidinous butterfly become, without their

knowledge, accomplices in everything… You were warned.

Gastric reflux and the spirit of lucre are found in the mean smiles

of green technicians. All this so that cellophane-wrapped could shell

elytra mimic lustful outpourings – under the watchful eye of a fickle

trader. The fifty women who count the most take advantage

of their coffee break to gossip, while sinful Independent

Republicans caress a blissful cow, the one that meows... And all

that, again because of glorious screwdrivers and their

few exotic tastes Apericubes. *Nom de Dieu*, how could a dystopian

computer lie on wallpapers in the middle of St-Patrick's Day (March

17th) ?!? And of course hoteliers – all on their gums – they broke

Peru's momentum, despite one of the queen's porcelain services.

Meanwhile, under your seat, the divine blue buccaneer was

squealing sweet melodies (yes, that's true, only when your

rooster wasn't exactly square, but still...).

Intermezzo 11

... los *curtains of life; the sun darkened, still warm on the autocratic seas;*

grainy cosmos watched over by three obedient corpses; this titanium

operating table; water locked on the E string (low); Place Blanche, black

with people; a mouth open like an oven (nuts come out); a baby lemonade

under the low balcony forehead (teeth clashing there in the 'hecto-chrome'

plane); all those cars advancing in colonnades under my window; five

sequins from the sphinx; the humble cake with a concave

smile (a ventilator becomes its refuge)...

And a toy soldier sinking straight into the vague

wasteland, and all the subtle windy dreams, crucified ad nauseam...

Well, all that is nothing compared to the beauty of the alcoholic's shaking

hands, and necessity having its way. Dont acte ?... *Don't act !*

Epilogue

*(Retrospectively thinking about the rastaquouère
boxer and Lloyd's Bank agency – the one of
Cravans, Charente-Maritime)*

A mercyful but doting Louise Bourgeois-Bourgoin cut her teeth on

a tear-filled punk. Then, as far as any eye could see, she engulfed

the goalkeeper – all in order to get back to sleep – and the slender

pivot age. To escape boredom, a depressed billionaire then

drank seas for a friend who was dear to him (it was Léonie). Paul

Ricœur, after a severe crisis of uraemia, had written to him : "Do

you dream of electric sheep – and of their eyes which

dare not declare themselves to us ? ". On the other hand, waiting for

more, the shiny bitter fruits of summer have become embroiled in

mosquito's nets... And since I was not born a woman, it's

ok if I have become one now – by dint of getting drunk and filling

your too full men ! Anyway, from now on, the jellyfish and the

bookseller baboon will be responsible of the baker's innocence.

And, if we except mysteries of the

West, particular anxieties will be reserved for ribalds, rivers

included… Thus, yes yes, the Durruti brothers will dance with their

hairdressers, supported as they will be by unions of

all persuasions. But you know, it's a trap : at *la Ciudad*

Universitaria, the oldest will suffer a fatal gust

(coming from who knows where).

More than happy, Lucien Ginsburg is not able to see the pale

chronicles of Maurice Merleau-Ponty – in any kind of paintings.

Janitors in flip-flops have slipped away through the shadow of their

warm ginger rabbit, while headbands and a cake impose

their logic *in extremis*, at Mount Tabor's feet. Then, shamelessly,

the same two plus some psychedelic fishmongers step over the color

of my children. Proud thugs, staring blankly, consequently put up

for sale the shimmering ugly sow reserved for their descendants.

And then, refusing to lose hope, they lock themselves in the bubble

of poor singer Diam's. Yes, yes, same one from the Avignon

festival, festival which was created by the anti-pope

and his purple (although cursed) star.

Doubtful of his recent discovery, a left-wing hummingbird placed

an ad to elicit some inexpert opinions. So, the emerald green

Tuareg put his pit bull away – in a vegetable bin – and improvised

words as big as sheeps… But he finally showed himself

to be very little talkative, alleging that it would be necessary to have

recourse to Mitsubishi – and especially to Mitterrand,

the King of Kings . This semi-remarkable infinity finally proclaims

it : "In the brambles, my uncle and Jean Yanne go out in their

work clothes, with a tuned clock. That is to say : 40 centuries are

watching us, you dirty viper of the department store !" Still, our

badger next door is going to eat the unaware Earth,

with his Malaysian maid...

Ultimate problem : seating at the top of a gloomy pyramid, will

Tod Browning and Mimi Coutelier finally elect the 2 sausages

that our eight grandparents were eyeing ? And, on the

other hand, over Ultimate Governor's block, there is no point in

ignoring youth and its seven so sympathetic warts-lies... Not to

mention the fact that depressive popes and stubborn

snakes led themselves to confusion. Hence again, THE big issue is :

murder or a new religion ??... Oh by the way – I've been thinking –, three captains who passed through Lorraine discovered, lying on a

bed of nettles, the ebony black drums of my beating heart.

Subsequently they declined thirteen small

breviaries *à la* Aimé Césaire : soft tam-tams and pseudo-logical

long sausage (because not enough cows were found in it).

As for *Les Tontons Flingueurs*, like tradition dictates, they took

(and put) their hands on the juicy

idiot; *und jetzt* dance with Jolly Jumper (we clearly

can recognize the azure snot, the drool of eternity and the calf-that-

drank-the-air around their skirts). Anyway, Leo Frank & Leo

Frankel ? Françoise Dolto (born Marette) or Mary

Phagan (born in Marietta) ?? Or is it Lautéamont's wife plus

Evguéni Prigojine (actually Irving Berlin in gears

through jungles of ice) ??? Finally and

like always, six old betrayed men –

Erich von Stroheim stuck in the middle of his tide,

pretty clowns *à la* Chocolat and Arthur Schopenhauer's

four ties – continue to maintain a stormy relationship…

Yeeees, you're right : with the terrible bright

silversmith – precisely the one of

calle Camacua (Montevideo, Uruguay) !

Everywhere and nowhere
at the same time.
Stella-Plage/
Cambridge/
Iznajar/
Paris/
Bath,
July 2023

From the same author

« Paysages/Visages/Voyages : Un tour du monde en 100 photos »
(Ed. BoD – 2012&2021 / ISBN 9-782322-409068)

- « Un air de famille - 500 célébrités qui se ressemblent »
(Ed. BoD – 2012)

- « Le Père-Lachaise, un cimetière bien vivant »
(Ed. BoD – 2013&2021 / ISBN 9-782322-216734)

- « Ils ont dit… »
(Ed. BoD – 2013)

- « Aphorismes, paradoxes et autres billevesées »
(Ed. BoD – 2014 / ISBN 9-782322-185276)

- « Sentences sans queue ni tête (La beauté du non-sens) »
(Ed. BoD – 2014 / ISBN 9-782322-193134)

- « Qui est qui ? - Dictionnaire de pseudonymes »
(Ed. BoD – 2014 / ISBN 9-782322-205240)

- « Dictionnaire de la guerre civile espagnole et de ses prémices
1930-1939 »   (Ed. BoD – 2015 / ISBN 9-782322-193219)

- « Absurdomanies… »
(Ed. Bookelis – 2015)

- « Les fins mots de la fin »
(Ed. BoD – 2016 / ISBN 9-782322-201709)

- « Villages de France »
(Ed. Bookelis – 2016)

- « Aphorismes, paradoxes et autres calembredaines »
(Ed. BoD – 2017 / ISBN 9-782322-224333)

- « Last words, last words… out ! »
(Ed. Bookelis – 2017 & Ed. BoD 2017 / ISBN Ebook 9-782322-210183)

- « Mon Paris insolite »
(Ed. BoD – 2018 / ISBN 9-782322-115297)

- « Apprenez l'anglais entre faux-amis »
(Ed. BoD – 2019 / ISBN Ebook 9-782322-238712)

- « Une année de hasards exquis et de cadavres objectifs »
(Ed. BoD – 2019 / ISBN 9-782322-209972)

- « Aphorismes, paradoxes et autres carabistouilles »
(Ed. BoD – 2020 / ISBN 9-782322-255986)

- « Mon Paris insolite (et illustré) »
(Ed. BoD – 2020&2022 / ISBN 9-782322-423439)

- « Dictionnaire des rues de Paris »
(Ed. BoD – 2020 / ISBN 9-782322-260027)

- « Aphorismes, paradoxes et autres fariboles »
(Ed. BoD – 2021 / ISBN 9-782322-394845)

- « Dark Syd of the Floyd (Les deux vies de Roger K. Barrett) »
(Ed. BoD – 2021 / ISBN 9-782322-396061)

- « Communes de France aux noms insolites »
(Ed. BoD – 2021 / ISBN 9-782322-412884)

- « Photomontages I »
(Ed. BoD – 2022 / ISBN 9-782322-411405)

- « Une banale histoire d'amour du temps jadis »
(Ed. BoD – 2022 / ISBN 9-782322-393398)

« Aphorismes, paradoxes et autres fumisteries »
(Ed. BoD – 2022 / ISBN 9-782322-393312)

- « 500 celebrities who look alike (A family resemblance) »
(Ed. BoD – 2022 / ISBN 9-782322-411658)

- « Gargouilles et marmousets dans la sculpture médiévale »
(Ed. Bookelis – 2018 & BoD – 2022 / ISBN 9-782322-432394)

- « Je suis un être délicat »
(Ed. BoD – 2023 / ISBN 9-782322-454839)

- « Photomontages II »
(Ed. BoD – 2023 / ISBN 9-782322-130979)

« Aphorismes, paradoxes et autres niaiseries »
(Ed. BoD – 2023 / ISBN 9-782322-472666)

August 2023- MiguelSydRuiz
www.miguelsydruiz.jimdo.com
www.bod.fr

August 2023 - MiguelSydRuiz

www.miguelsydruiz.jimdo.com

www.bod.fr